LOST!

by Roxanne Heide
and Florence Parry Heide

illustrated by William S. Shields

HOLT, RINEHART AND WINSTON, INC.
New York / Toronto / London / Sydney

A SATELLITE BOOK

Satellite Books are supplementary units designed
for individualized, independent reading to accom-
pany THE HOLT BASIC READING SYSTEM,
by Eldonna L. Evertts, Lyman C. Hunt, and
Bernard J. Weiss.

GENERAL EDITORS
SATELLITE BOOKS

Lyman C. Hunt
Patricia Hynes Estill

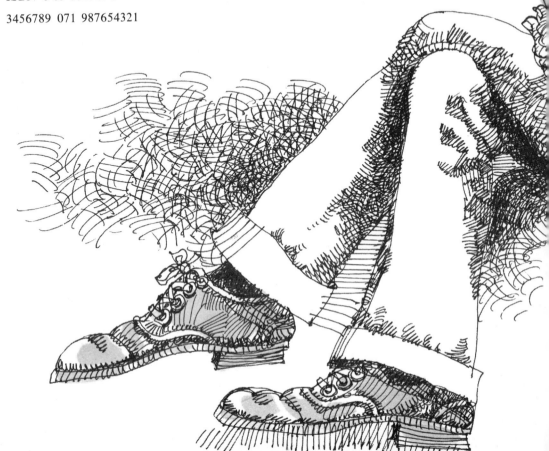

I always play detective. You know, I like finding clues and figuring out things. For instance, on the train I was pretending to be a secret agent. I kept my eye on a suspicious-looking man across from me. I pretended that he was a diamond smuggler and that I couldn't let him out of my sight. But I forgot about him in a hurry when I found out my wallet was lost.

I had it when the conductor came to take the tickets. That had been two hours before. I remember taking out my wallet when the conductor asked for my ticket. He smiled at me and said, "All on your own, eh?"

I wasn't really alone. After all, Mom and Dad saw me off at the station in Hudson and Uncle Bob and Aunt Sally were going to meet me in Waubesha. Then we were going on a fishing trip. I could hardly wait. Uncle Bob was the best fisherman in the world. No, I really wasn't exactly on my own.

That's what I thought, then.

But now my wallet was gone. I had to find it in a hurry. The train would be in Waubesha pretty soon. It wasn't in my jacket. It wasn't on the seat beside me. It wasn't on the floor. Where else could I look?

I looked at the man across from me. For one minute I let myself pretend he had stolen my wallet to find out if I was a secret agent. Now I had to figure out a way to steal it back.

I stood up. I decided I'd better stop playing and find my wallet. I looked up and down the aisle. Maybe I dropped it on the floor and someone coming by had kicked it under a seat. I walked up and down through all the cars looking for it. I went from one end of the train to the other. People stared at me. I didn't want to ask if they had seen my wallet. They might think I was accusing them of taking it.

The train started to slow down. I heard the conductor call, "Waubesha, Waubesha! Next stop Chicago!" Everything was happening so fast! I'd have to get off the train without my wallet. Without my money.

Wait a minute. Where was my suitcase? Which car had I been in? I ran through the cars, bumping into the people who were waiting to get off the train. There it was. I was just picking up my suitcase when the train started to move again.

I had to signal Uncle Bob so he'd know I was trapped on the train. I ran to a window. Too late! The station was already behind us.

I sat down. It felt like the end of the world. I looked out of the window and tried to think.

Uncle Bob and Aunt Sally would call my parents. They'd all know I missed the stop. They'd figure out some way to get me back to Waubesha. I'd call as soon as I got to Chicago.

But what about my wallet? It had to be somewhere. I looked through my jacket again. I felt something. No, it was not my wallet. But what was it?

I took out three envelopes. Where did they come from? Then I remembered. Mrs. Baker had handed them to me earlier that morning. She's the lady across the street. She always takes care of Mom's African violets and picks up the mail when we're away. A sort of plant baby-sitter, I guess.

My parents and I had been visiting some friends. They have a kid my age and we had fun. We stayed a couple of extra days and got home late last night. Then this morning, I had been rushing around getting ready for my fishing trip. I ran over to Mrs. Baker's to pick up Mom's plants and the mail. I stuck the letters in my pocket since I needed both hands for the plants, and then I forgot all about them.

4

Two of the letters were bills or ads or something. It was the third envelope I now looked at twice. It was addressed to Mom and Dad and to me, too. I wondered what it could be. I opened it. It was a letter from Aunt Sally written on yellow note paper. The postmark said Chicago, and it had been sent a few days before.

I only half read it then. Later I would read and reread it for the important clues it held. The words that really hit me were "change of plans." I raced through the letter.

Last minute urgent business meeting in Chicago . . . the fishing trip will be a few days late. . . .

I put the letter down. Uncle Bob had not been waiting for me in Waubesha. He and Aunt Sally were somewhere in Chicago, but they didn't even say where.

Mom and Dad thought I was with Uncle Bob. Uncle Bob and Aunt Sally thought I was at home.

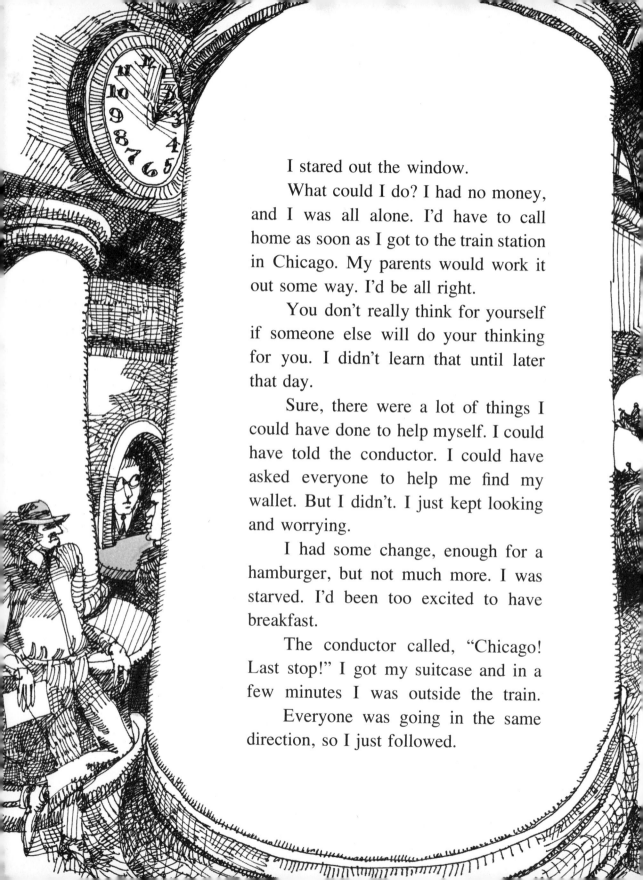

I stared out the window.

What could I do? I had no money, and I was all alone. I'd have to call home as soon as I got to the train station in Chicago. My parents would work it out some way. I'd be all right.

You don't really think for yourself if someone else will do your thinking for you. I didn't learn that until later that day.

Sure, there were a lot of things I could have done to help myself. I could have told the conductor. I could have asked everyone to help me find my wallet. But I didn't. I just kept looking and worrying.

I had some change, enough for a hamburger, but not much more. I was starved. I'd been too excited to have breakfast.

The conductor called, "Chicago! Last stop!" I got my suitcase and in a few minutes I was outside the train.

Everyone was going in the same direction, so I just followed.

I found myself in the biggest room
I had ever seen in my whole life.

I looked around for the telephones. The hamburger would come after that.

I carried my suitcase over to a telephone booth and sat down.

I took a dime out of my pocket and dialed the operator. "Collect call, please." I waited. Mom and Dad would figure something out. The phone rang and rang.

Then the operator came on, "I'm sorry, there's no answer."

I stared at the telephone. "No answer!"

I hung up and looked around the station. I was all alone. I tried to laugh at myself—all alone with a couple of hundred people around! But that's the loneliest kind of lonely. I found that out then.

I sat on the stool in the telephone booth and tried to think. I'd call my parents later. They'd be home then. Maybe. Suddenly I saw a man standing nearby. He was staring at me angrily. Why? What had I done? Then I knew. He was just waiting for the telephone!

I'd better start moving. I had to think for myself. I had to get home. That was the only thing to do. A ticket. That's what I needed. Just as I was heading for the ticket counter two things hit me at the same time. Thing one—the thought that tickets cost money. Thing two—a little boy who ran right into me.

Benjee

"Benjeeeeeeeeee!" someone called.

I saw a lady holding a baby and calling to the boy who had run into me. He was already off in another direction. I turned around to chase the little boy and tripped over my suitcase. But I picked it up and carried it with me. I wasn't going to lose anything else.

I caught the boy and led him back to his mother. "Thanks so much," she said, smiling at me. "It's hard to look after both kids at once." Then she took a quarter out of her purse and gave it to me.

I started to shake my head, but then I stared
at it, smiled at it, and took it. That was an idea! I
could make the money for my ticket home. There
would be other kids running off in all directions in
that big waiting room. Other mothers would be
happy to rest for a minute and let me watch the
children.

I thanked the lady, turned around, and fell
flat on my face. I hadn't seen the suitcase—again.
I couldn't keep dragging it around and tripping over
it. Not if I was going to be running after kids.

I had seen other people put their suitcases in lockers. I walked over to a row of them. The locker cost me twenty-five cents, but I had to do it. Then I got another idea. No one liked dragging suitcases around. I could help carry people's luggage. I could make money that way, too.

I looked around the station at all the people — almost all of them were carrying something. I could surely make enough to buy my ticket home.

But it wasn't easy. Hardly anyone wanted my help. Or sometimes they let me carry their luggage and all I got was a big thank you. I didn't ask for money, but I didn't turn it down either.

Between times I called home. Still no answer.

It was taking so long to make money. If only I hadn't lost that wallet.

I thought a minute. What about the Lost and Found booth? Maybe someone had found my wallet and turned it in. It was worth a try, anyway. The lady looked at me as I walked up to the counter.

"May I help you?" she asked.

"I really hope so," I said. "I lost my wallet on the train."

"What is your name and address? What did your wallet look like?" she asked.

I gave her all the information.

"We did have your wallet," said the lady. "The conductor brought it in and we sent it out to your home."

"Oh," I said. "Well, thanks anyway."

I turned away. At least that solved the mystery of the missing wallet. But it didn't help me to get home. I walked over to the ticket counter. Maybe I had earned enough money by now. "How much is a one-way ticket to Hudson, please?" I asked. "And when does the train leave?"

The man pushed his glasses up on his nose. "Let's see. A ticket costs five dollars. And the next train to Hudson leaves tomorrow afternoon at four o'clock."

"Oh," I said. It seemed to me I was always saying "oh."

Now I didn't know what to do. I couldn't get home that night. I didn't know where to reach my parents. And I didn't know how to find Uncle Bob and Aunt Sally. All I knew for sure was that they were here in Chicago.

It was like looking for a needle in a haystack. Or was it?

I sat down on a bench in the waiting room and took Aunt Sally's letter out of my pocket. This time I really read it.

We can see Lake Michigan from our fifth floor room at the hotel.

There couldn't be too many hotels in Chicago that were that close to the lake.

I read on.

Remember Ruth Adams? She just had a new baby, and today I walked over to the hospital to see her. It was a nice walk, but on the way back I got caught in the rain.

Okay. It was a hotel that was close to Lake Michigan and close to a hospital. That made it easier. But I needed a map.

I stood up, put the letter in my pocket, and walked over to a newsstand.

"Where can I get a map of Chicago?" I asked the man behind the counter.

He looked at me. "I can sell you a big one for a quarter."

He must have seen my face fall. "That's for rich guys," he said. "You can get a little one for nothing. It's on the back of a magazine that tells you about the fancy restaurants you can go to if you're a millionaire. Here."

He handed me a little magazine and flipped it over to the back. Sure enough, there was a map. Not too hard. I could figure it out.

"Thanks a lot," I said, and he waved me off.

I wasn't sure if I could find the right hotel, but I was going to try. The map showed the main streets and where Lake Michigan was. It showed the railway station, so I could figure out where I was. I sat with the telephone directory, the map, Aunt Sally's letter, and some dimes.

I looked in the phone book for the hotels. Then I looked up the addresses on the map. Then I looked up hospitals and checked those with the map.

It took a long time. Finally I had the names of five hotels that were close enough to Lake Michigan so you could see it from a room on the fifth floor. And near enough to a hospital so you could walk there — on high heels, I thought to myself, remembering Aunt Sally.

I took a deep breath. I made the first call to the Sussex East Hotel.

"Hello, do you have a Mr. and Mrs. Robert Sayres there, please?"

"I'm sorry, Ma'am, we do not have them listed as guests."

Operators always call me Ma'am. My voice is kind of high.

I made the next call to the Lake Terrace Hotel. When I asked for Mr. or Mrs. Sayres, the lady at the other end asked me how to spell their name.

"S-A-Y-R-E-S." I said.

"F as in Frank?" she asked.

"No," I said. "S as in soup and sandwich." I was really hungry. It seemed to take forever for her to find out what name I was spelling. They weren't registered there.

I looked around the station before I put my next dime in. It looked bigger than it had at the beginning. The station, I mean. The dime looked smaller.

I began to picture what it would seem like when the last hotel on my list had no guests named Sayres. I called two more. No luck.

The last one was the Claridge Hotel. I finished dialing and crossed my fingers.

"Hello," I said. "Do you have a Mr. and Mrs. Sayres staying there?"

After a hundred years a voice said, "Yes, we do have a Mr. and Mrs. Sayres. May I connect you?"

"Yes!" I thought I shouted, but it came out more of a squeak.

She rang once, four, ten times. Then she said, "The party does not answer."

I didn't know what to say. "Thanks a lot." I said finally and hung up.

I stood up and stared at the telephone. Then I thought of a plan.

All I had to do was go to that hotel and wait until they came back. Then everything would be all right. I looked at the map. I'd have to take a taxi. I counted my money. I still had eighty cents. That should be plenty.

I'd get my suitcase and go to the hotel and wait for them. Everything was so simple. At least that is what I thought then, at 4:05 P.M. What could go wrong?

A lot, I found out later.

I got my suitcase. As I was leaving, I waved at the man who had given me the map. He waved back. He had been the start of my good luck, I thought, and now all the worry was over. I was going to see Aunt Sally and Uncle Bob and everything was going to be all right.

I followed the signs that said TAXIS, and before I knew it I was sitting in a taxicab.

But where was I going? Had I left my notes and the addresses and the names of the hotels in my pocket or in the telephone booth?

I checked. They were in my pocket. Whew! I leaned forward and said, "The Claridge Hotel, please," and then I sat back and breathed for the first time in a thousand hours. At least that's the way it seemed.

"First nice day all week," said the taxi driver.

"Yeah," I said.

I leaned forward about two minutes later to look at the moneymeter that was clicking off my hard-earned dimes.

"Eighty cents!" I yelled into the taxi driver's ear. "Let me out, right here! This is just where I want to go."

"Right here? I thought you wanted to go to the Claridge."

"I changed my mind," I said. "I just thought of something. Besides, I like to walk."

He stopped and I paid him. I didn't even have a dime left for a phone call.

I got out and set my suitcase on the sidewalk. I was near a very tall skyscraper. It had to be the tallest building in Chicago. I read the street signs. Then I took a look at the map.

I had a long way to go. So I started walking. The suitcase felt heavier and heavier. I wished I'd left it in the locker, but it was too late to think about that. I kept shifting it from one arm to the other. After a while, instead of one arm hurting, they both hurt. I walked and walked and walked.

Then I saw the sign: THE CLARIDGE. I said the name out loud. It sounded like the most beautiful name in the world. It looked like the most beautiful building in the world. I almost ran the rest of the way.

I flew up these stairs and into the lobby. My feet hurt, my arms hurt, my head hurt, but I felt great.

"Mr. and Mrs. Sayres, please," I said. I was almost shouting.

The man at the desk turned away for a minute. Then he turned back and said, "Sorry, they've checked out."

"Checked out!" I said it out loud and then I said it to myself a couple of times. I couldn't believe it.

"Where did they go?" I asked.

He shrugged. "I don't know, but I do remember the lady said they would be able to see the whole city since it was such a nice evening."

The telephone rang and the man turned away to answer it.

"Oh," I said. There wasn't much else to say. I took my suitcase and sat down there in the lobby. I'd missed them. What would I do now? I had no money. Not even a dime for a phone call.

I sat there feeling sorry for myself for a while. I thought of all the people I could have asked to help me right from the beginning. There was the conductor. I could have waited and told him about my wallet, or I could have gone straight to the Lost and Found booth. All along the way there were people who could have helped. But I wanted to prove I could do it alone.

I sat there staring into space. I'd been in such a hurry I hadn't used my head. Why hadn't I left a message when I first called the Claridge? Then Aunt Sally and Uncle Bob would have waited for me.

But wait a minute! The man at the desk said Aunt Sally had mentioned being able to see the whole city. Something rang a bell. I reached into my pocket for the letter.

I glanced through it again. There — that's what I was looking for.

There's a restaurant not far from here that's way up on the top floor of the tallest building in town. We're waiting for the first clear day or evening — and then up we go for an elegant dinner and a super-elegant view! We just can't leave Chicago until we've done that!

I thought of what the taxi driver had said. "First nice day all week." They were there. They had to be. Up at the top of that skyscraper. I passed it on the way.

I stood up and reached for my suitcase. The minute I picked it up I knew I didn't want to have it with me on this trip.

I walked over to the desk. "Can I leave my suitcase here for a while?" I asked.

"Sure," said the man. Then he looked at me.

"Anything I can do to help?" he asked. I shook my head. I could handle this alone.

I ran out of the hotel and back the way I had come. There it was. That had to be it—that great black skyscraper just over there.

But it was not just over there. I kept walking and walking. The building didn't seem to get any closer. In fact, it seemed to get farther away.

Why hadn't I asked about the restaurant at the hotel? I could have called. The man at the desk had been willing to help—but again I'd been so sure I could do it myself. It was too late now. I was so out of breath I didn't think I could walk another step. But I knew I had to.

Somehow, I got there. I looked up at the building. It was so high I nearly fell over. Which door? There were so many! I just picked one and ran through it. A man in uniform was standing near some elevators.

"I have to go up to the restaurant," I said.

"Okay, sonny, step in. You sure must be hungry to be in such a hurry."

The minute he said "hungry," I realized how starved I was. When the elevator started moving up, I thought my stomach would fall right through the floor. It must have been going a hundred miles an hour.

And then, there we were at the restaurant. This was really my very last chance. But what if they weren't here? I couldn't think about that. They had to be here. I rushed up to the man with the menus.

"One, sir?" he asked, lifting his eyebrows.

I took a deep breath. "I just want to look for someone," I said. I knew I wasn't much to look at, so I put all the importance I could into my voice.

The man frowned. "My aunt and uncle," I said. "They're here."

I ran past him into the middle of the dining room. I went from one table to the next.

People looked up at me. The man with the menus caught up with me.

I ran past him again. Then I saw them. I saw Uncle Bob and Aunt Sally. I really saw them!

I don't know what they thought when they saw me. I know I was smiling so hard I thought my jaw would break.

Aunt Sally jumped up. "What on earth! How did you ever . . ."

Uncle Bob stared at me, blinking his eyes.

"Just call me Detective Morgan," I said. I looked out of the window. You really could see the whole city. "Hungry Detective Morgan," I added.

Uncle Bob called to a waiter standing nearby. "A menu for Detective Morgan, please," he said, still blinking his eyes at me.

I knew there would be plenty of time to tell them that I really had been a detective. But right then all I could think about was the mountain of food I was going to eat before I told my story!